7

Matt Christopher®

All Keyed Up

Text by Stephanie Peters
Illustrated by Daniel Vasconcellos

LITTLE, BROWN AND COMPANY

New York · An AOL Time Warner Company

First Paperback Edition

Library of Congress Cataloging-in-Publication Data

Peters, Stephanie True.
    All keyed up / Matt Christopher; illustrated by Daniel Vasconcellos ; text by Stephanie Peters. —1st ed.
        p.   cm.—(Soccer 'Cats ; #7)
    Summary: When his soccer teammate and new friend Stookie asks him to take care of his gerbils while he is on vacation, Jerry is happy to agree, but then disaster strikes.
    ISBN 0-316-69241-7 (hc)/ISBN 0-316-73821-2 (pb)
    [1. Soccer—Fiction. 2. Responsibility—Fiction.
3. Friendship—Fiction. 4. Gerbils—Fiction.] I. Christopher, Matt. II. Vasconcellos, Daniel, ill. III. Title.

PZ7.P441835 Al 2002
[Fic]—dc21   2001038115

                    HC: 10 9 8 7 6 5 4 3 2 1
                    PB: 10 9 8 7 6 5 4 3 2 1

                            WOR (hc)

                          COM-MO (pb)

              Printed in the United States of America

Soccer 'Cats Team Roster

Lou Barnes	*Striker*
Jerry Dinh	*Striker*
Stookie Norris	*Striker*
Dewey London	*Halfback*
Bundy Neel	*Halfback*
Amanda Caler	*Halfback*
Brant Davis	*Fullback*
Lisa Gaddy	*Fullback*
Ted Gaddy	*Fullback*
Alan Minter	*Fullback*
Bucky Pinter	*Goalie*

Subs:

Jason Shearer

Dale Tuget

Roy Boswick

Edith "Eddie" Sweeny

Chapter 1

Here! Send it here!" Jerry Dinh called. He pounded down the field, looking for a pass from his fellow striker and Soccer 'Cats teammate Stookie Norris.

Stookie glanced up. With a quick jab, he sent the ball bouncing to Jerry.

Jerry and a Panther halfback ran to meet it. Jerry beat the halfback by a step. He controlled the ball and started dribbling as fast as he could toward the Panther goal.

The halfback didn't give up, however. She chased Jerry, determined to steal the ball.

Jerry did his best to protect the ball. But the Panther was all over him. Jerry had to pass the ball back to Stookie.

Stookie caught it on his chest and let it drop to the ground at his feet. Then he paused.

The Panther defense moved in.

Oh, no! Jerry groaned to himself. *Stookie's going to get slaughtered!*

But Stookie didn't. Just as the first Panther reached him, he darted to the left, bringing the ball with him. The Panther ran by him, a surprised look on his face. As the second Panther lunged forward, Stookie moved right. The second Panther ended up on the ground.

"Go, Stookie, go!" Jerry and his teammates shouted. Stookie dodged the last defender. He had a clear shot at the goal! The goalie rushed out to meet him. Stookie faked left. When the goalie moved to block the shot, Stookie darted right and slammed the ball into the net.

Jerry bounced on his toes, grinning with glee. "All right, Stookie!" he shouted.

Two minutes later the game ended. The final score was 'Cats 2, Panthers 1.

Jerry was grabbing his sweatshirt off the bench when someone tapped him on the shoulder. He looked up to see Stookie.

Jerry's family had moved in to the house next to Stookie's a month ago. Jerry had hoped that he and Stookie would get to know each other better. But it hadn't happened, at least not yet. In fact, sometimes Stookie made Jerry nervous. Stookie could be prickly and hot-tempered.

Now, however, he looked happy. "Great pass you made at the end," Stookie said.

"Thanks," Jerry replied, grinning at Stookie. "Great goal you made at the end!"

Stookie laughed. "You want to walk home together?" he asked.

"Sure," Jerry answered. The two boys headed off the field toward their neighborhood.

They chatted about the game, then Stookie said, "Did Coach Bradley tell you that you're taking my position at center next game?"

Jerry was surprised. "I am? Why?"

"My family is going away for three days, so I'm going to miss the game." Stookie stopped. "Can I ask you a favor? Could you take care of my gerbils while we're gone?"

Jerry nodded. "Just tell me what I have to do."

"It'd be easier if I showed you. Can you sleep over tonight?"

Jerry agreed to ask his folks.

Cool! Jerry thought. *Maybe Stookie wants to be better friends with me, too!*

Chapter 2

Mrs. Dinh helped Jerry pack his pajamas, his toothbrush, and a change of clothes for the next day.

"Don't forget Otter," she reminded him.

Otter was a puppet Jerry's dad had brought him all the way from California. He was big and soft and had a hole in the back where you stuck your hand to make the arms move. Jerry slept with him every night.

But should he bring him to Stookie's house? What if Stookie made fun of him?

"Uh, I don't know, Mom," Jerry said.

"Why don't you pack him, just in case?" his mother suggested. "You know what I always say: Better to have him and not need him than to need him and not have him."

Jerry smiled. "Okay," he said, sticking Otter into his knapsack. He shut off his bedroom light, and together they walked downstairs.

"Have fun!" Mrs. Dinh called as Jerry walked the short way to Stookie's house.

"Come on in!" Stookie said when he answered the door. Jerry said hello to Stookie's parents, then the two boys hurried upstairs to Stookie's room.

Stookie pushed open the door with a grand gesture. "What do you think?"

"Cool!" Jerry cried. And he meant it. Stookie's room was covered with sports posters and banners. One bed had sheets with soccer balls on it, the other had basketballs. But the neatest thing was the structure in the corner. It was three levels high and enclosed with clear plastic. Plastic tubes led up to each level

where there were wheels, platforms, and other things to climb on.

"What is that?" he asked.

"That's where my gerbils live," Stookie said proudly. Jerry looked closer. Sure enough, one gerbil was scurrying up a tube. The other was buried in the wood shavings that lined the bottom.

"Gerbils are pretty easy to take care of, and they're really fun to watch," Stookie continued. "All you have to do is make sure they have enough water in their bottles and food in their trays. I usually fill the water at night and the food in the morning."

He lifted the mesh top of the cage and pulled out a bottle. He showed Jerry how to fill it, then returned it to its holder. "Just make sure you close this top," Stookie warned as he lowered the mesh cover. "If these guys get out, they can make a mess."

"Gotcha," Jerry said. "What are their names?"

"That's Peanut Butter," Stookie said, pointing to the climbing gerbil. "Marshmallow is the one sleeping."

"Are they boys or girls?"

"Boys. Mom made sure when we bought them." Stookie grinned. "She didn't want any baby gerbils in the house, she said."

"That's right." Jerry and Stookie looked up to see Mrs. Norris in the doorway. "You boys ready to come have some popcorn and watch a movie?"

"You betcha!" the boys chorused. They left the room, Jerry taking one last look at the gerbil habitat.

I'll take good care of you guys, he promised the animals silently.

Chapter 3

After the movie and popcorn, Jerry and Stookie got into their pajamas, brushed their teeth, and climbed into bed. Jerry hesitated for a minute, then reached to the floor for his knapsack.

"Stookie, will you laugh at me if—" He hesitated.

"If what?" Stookie said sleepily.

"If I sleep with a stuffed animal?" Jerry held his breath.

Stookie chuckled. "I won't if you won't!"

That's when Jerry saw that Stookie had a special toy, too. His was shaped like a snowman.

Jerry pulled Otter from the knapsack. From his bed, he could see out the window to his own room. He could see the stars, too.

"The stars look cool tonight, don't they?" he murmured to Stookie.

Stookie grunted. "You like looking at stars?"

"Yeah," said Jerry. "I've got a telescope in my room so I can see them up close."

Stookie rolled over and looked at him. "Really? Can I see it sometime?"

"Sure!" Jerry said. He gave Otter a squeeze. Soon both boys were asleep.

The next morning, Jerry packed up his pajamas, yesterday's clothes, his toothbrush, and Otter. He and Stookie ate a big stack of pancakes for breakfast. Then Jerry practiced filling the gerbils' water bottles.

"See?" Stookie said. "Easy as pie." He reached into his pocket and pulled out a key. It was on a small ring with a tag that said

"Norris." "Here's the key to the house. Just make sure you lock the door when you leave."

"I will," Jerry promised. He slipped the key into his knapsack.

Stookie suggested that they round up some of the other 'Cats for a game of soccer. Half an hour later, eight 'Cats showed up at the field, ready to play.

Stookie and Bundy Neel were elected captains.

"Who's got a coin to flip to see who chooses first?" Bundy asked.

"I think I've got one in my knapsack," Jerry said. He dug around and came up with a dime. Stookie won the toss. He chose Amanda Caler. Bundy took Dewey London. Stookie picked Jerry, and Bundy pointed to Lisa Gaddy. Stookie chose Jason Shearer.

"Guess I know where I'm going," Ted Gaddy grumbled as he joined his twin sister.

"Let the games begin!" Jason cried, flinging his baseball cap in the air.

"Stop horsing around and get in the goal," growled Stookie.

Jason bowed. "At your service," he said. He dodged Stookie's punch and jogged backward to the goal as the rest of the 'Cats laughed.

Jerry laughed, too. He was surprised that Stookie had chosen Jason. When it came to soccer, Stookie was all business, even if it was just a pickup game played for fun.

The game started. Since Stookie had had first choice of players, Bundy's team got the ball first. Bundy toed the ball over to Dewey. Dewey started downfield, dribbling swiftly.

Stookie charged him. In the blink of an eye, he'd stolen the ball and made it halfway toward the opposite goal. Lisa jumped forward, but Stookie dodged past her. Ted hopped like a frog in front of the goal, trying to guess where Stookie would shoot.

He guessed wrong. Stookie faked left, but he shot right when Ted went for the fake. Goal!

His teammates gathered round to congratulate Stookie. But Stookie impatiently waved them back to their positions.

"It's only one goal," he reminded them. "They could still beat us!"

"Oh, lighten up, Stookie," Jason drawled. "It's just a silly practice game."

Stookie's temper flared up. "If it's so silly to you," he cried, "then why don't you just leave?!"

Jason just shrugged and strolled back to the goal. Stookie watched him with narrow eyes.

Man, Jerry thought to himself. *I sure would hate to get on Stookie's bad side!*

Chapter 4

The practice game continued. This time, Dewey started with the ball. The minute he touched it, Stookie raced forward to try to steal it. Jerry positioned himself between Dewey and Bundy, ready to grab the ball if Dewey passed it.

But Dewey surprised them. Instead of sending it sideways to Bundy, he knocked it backward to Lisa.

Lisa controlled the ball, then darted down the field, dribbling madly. Amanda squared off against her, and Lisa almost lost the ball.

But she recovered and with a quick move sent the ball rocketing toward the goal.

Jason ran out to meet it, but it took a strange bounce over his outstretched hands and into the goal.

"Whoops," Jason said, shrugging. He retrieved the ball and handed it to Stookie. Stookie didn't say a word, but the glare he gave Jason was withering. Jason just stared back, chewing his gum, until Stookie walked back to the center of the field.

After that, Stookie was unstoppable. He scored three more goals single-handedly before Bundy's team scored their second one. When Bundy did finally get it into the net, Stookie shouted at Jason for not having played better. Jerry cringed, but Jason just rolled his eyes and told Stookie to lay off.

Finally, when the score was eight to three, Bundy's team had had enough.

"Let's go down to the town pool!" Ted suggested.

"Yeah, maybe Stookie can cool off his hot head there!" Jason said.

Stookie grinned. "Aw, come on, Jason," he said. "You know my bark is worse than my bite. Anyway, I can't go to the pool. My folks and I are leaving for our trip this afternoon."

"How about you, Jerry?" Lisa asked.

"Sure, I'll meet you guys there after lunch." Everyone agreed that was a good plan. Stookie and Jerry walked home together.

"Hey, have fun with your folks this weekend," Jerry said as they parted to go to their houses.

"I will. And have fun at the pool. Just make sure you're back in time to feed my gerbils," Stookie warned.

Jerry patted his knapsack. "I've got the key right in here. Nothing to worry about."

"I hope not," Stookie said as he climbed the steps into his house. "If anything happened to those gerbils, I don't know what I'd do."

Jerry gulped.

Chapter 5

What had Stookie meant by that? Jerry wondered as he hurried to his room to get his swim things. *Aw, he was probably just joking around. Like he said, his bark is worse than his bite. Not that I have to worry about that, because nothing is going to go wrong!*

He emptied his knapsack out on his bed. He was stuffing a beach towel and bathing suit into it when his mother called up.

"Jerry! Please bring your dirty clothes downstairs so I can wash them!"

"Okay, Mom!" Jerry replied. He gathered

up the clothes and headed downstairs. "I'm going to the pool after lunch, okay?"

"Sure," she said. She looked out the window. "I see Stookie's not going. He and his family just pulled out of the driveway with a car full of camping gear."

"Yeah, they're gone for three days," Jerry said. "I'm taking care of Stookie's gerbils."

"That's a big responsibility," his mother said. Then she frowned. "Are they leaving their house unlocked for three days?" she asked.

"No," Jerry said. "Stookie gave me a key."

"Well, you better put it in a safe place, then," his mother advised.

"Good idea," Jerry said. He hurried back to his room and looked through his knapsack. It was empty!

That's funny, Jerry thought nervously. *I'm sure I put the key in here this morning.*

He checked all the pockets. Nothing.

Maybe it's tangled up in the clothes! He raced

back to the washing machine, pulled over a chair, and lifted the lid. He plunged his arms into the warm, soapy water and started pulling clothes out.

"What are you doing?" his mother yelled from behind him. Startled, Jerry whipped around, sending a stream of water drops over the floor. He looked from the shirt in his hand to the pile of dripping clothes on the floor.

"Sorry, Mom! Sorry!" he cried. "I—I can't find the key to Stookie's house. I know I put it in my knapsack, but now it's not there. I thought it might have gotten caught in my pajamas or clothes or something." He lifted his sodden pajama top out of the wash. "But I can't find it here, either."

His mother shook her head. "I always give your clothes a good shake before I put them in the wash. I didn't find a key."

Jerry dropped the wet top back into the wash.

His mother ruffled his hair. "Now, don't

worry. Think about where the key might have fallen out of your knapsack."

Jerry's head snapped up. "The soccer field!" he cried. "Stookie and I went right to the field from his house! I bet it fell out on the way, or when I was looking for that coin!"

"The best way to find something you've misplaced is to retrace your steps," his mother said. "I'll clean up this mess. You go find that key!"

Chapter 6

Jerry set off at a trot for the soccer field. He scanned the sidewalks, streets, and grass along the way. Once he saw something gleaming in the grass, but it turned out to be a bottle cap.

"Nuts!" he said, winging the cap into a nearby trash can. When he reached the field, he was relieved to see it was empty. At least he could look around without having to wait for people to clear off.

Not that it would have mattered. Twenty minutes of careful searching turned up nothing but one of the wrappers from Jason's gum and the dime they'd used for the coin toss.

He walked back home in a gloom. Up in his room, he pulled the beach towel and bathing suit out of his knapsack and looked through it again, just in case. No key. Then, as he stared at the towel and suit, he had a thought.

He shoved the suit and towel back into the knapsack and rushed downstairs.

"Mom! I'm going to the pool!" he shouted.

"Did you find the key?"

"No, not yet! But maybe one of my friends did! And they're all going to be at the pool!"

"Okay, let's go," his mother said, emerging from the basement. "I made you a sandwich. You can eat it while I drive you there."

Jerry smiled gratefully. "Thanks, Mom. You're the best."

Jerry wolfed his sandwich down in the car. He didn't even care that he wasn't allowed in the pool for an hour after eating. He just wanted to get there to question his friends!

Most of them were already there. Jerry hurried over to them.

"Hi, guys! Listen, did any of you find a key on a ring with a name tag at the soccer field today?"

"A key?" Lisa said. "Not me. How about you, Ted?" Ted shook his head. One by one, the rest of the 'Cats did the same. Jerry's heart sank.

"Wait a minute," Bundy said. "Jason's not here yet. Maybe—"

He was cut off by a loud whoop. Seconds later, a huge wave of water crashed down over them all.

"Hi guys," Jason said, popping up with a grin. "Pretty decent cannonball, huh?" He ducked back under before anyone could answer.

Jerry followed him along the edge of the pool. When Jason came up for air, Jerry tapped him on the head.

"I hear you knocking, but you can't come

29

in!" Jason said, and he dove back under again. Jerry groaned and gave chase. After his third try, he finally got to ask Jason if he'd found a key.

"Nope!" was all Jason said before disappearing beneath the surface again.

Amanda sat down next to Jerry. "What's so important about this key?" she asked.

Jerry explained about the gerbils. Amanda chewed her lip.

"You know, those gerbils may be the least of your worries," she said.

"What do you mean?" Jerry asked.

"I mean, what if someone dishonest found that key? With that name tag on it, he could easily figure out what house it opened. And then . . ." Amanda shook her head.

Jerry swallowed hard. Amanda could be right, he realized. If a thief found the key, he could help himself to anything in the Norrises' house!

Chapter 7

The first thing Jerry did when he got home was search his house from top to bottom. Maybe he'd dropped the key somewhere. But no key showed up.

Then he went to Stookie's house. He stared at the outside, wondering if the key was lying on the floor inside. Maybe he should try prying open one of the windows. But no, he couldn't do that. He'd be no better than a thief himself if he sneaked into someone's house without permission.

But I do have their permission, he tried to reason

with himself. Still, he knew using a key to get in the front door was a lot different from breaking in through a window. He walked back to his house.

Dinner was a quiet affair that night. Mr. Dinh was away on business, and Jerry didn't feel much like talking. He turned on the TV after dinner, but didn't really pay attention to what was on. After a while, he decided he'd just go to bed.

If only I could be sure the gerbils were okay, he thought as he climbed the stairs. He slumped at his desk and stared out the window into Stookie's bedroom. He could see the gerbil habitat, but not the gerbils. They were too small.

Suddenly he sat up. He went to his other window, where his telescope was pointed at the sky. Carefully, he lifted the telescope off its stand and carried it to the window by his desk. He grabbed a pillow from his bed, laid it on the desk, and put the telescope on top of it. Then he leaned forward and looked through the eyepiece.

"Bingo!" he shouted. He could see everything in the gerbil habitat plain as day! There were the water bottles and the food trays. Both were nearly full still. Jerry breathed a sigh of relief.

Then he looked for the gerbils. Peanut Butter was running on a wheel. Jerry searched some more, but he couldn't find Marshmallow.

I'm sure he's sleeping in the wood shavings, Jerry thought hopefully. *Where else would he be?*

He was so happy the gerbils had enough food and water that he'd forgotten what Amanda had said at the pool. Her words came crashing back to him as he started to bring the telescope back to its stand.

Slowly, he laid the telescope back on the pillow.

I'll just have to stay awake tonight and keep an eye on their house, he said to himself. He changed into his pajamas and sat down at the desk again. He moved the telescope so that it was fixed on the Norrises' front door. Now, if anybody tried to go in, he'd be ready to catch him in the act.

Chapter 8

Sunlight spilled across Jerry's face, waking him with its warm brightness. He blinked. He'd fallen asleep in the chair!

"Oh, no!" he cried. Quickly, he looked through the telescope. Nothing seemed different from the night before. Everything seemed fine in Stookie's room, too. The gerbils' water bottles were half empty now, but the food trays were still full.

Jerry stood up and groaned. He was stiff all over from sleeping at the desk. He couldn't remember when he'd fallen asleep, but it must have been after two in the morning. That was the last time he'd looked at the clock.

Now it was nine o'clock. His stomach rumbled for breakfast. Jerry shook himself to get the last kinks out, then padded downstairs.

"Good morning, sleepyhead!" said his mother. "Still in your pajamas? Say, don't you have a soccer game this morning?"

Jerry slapped his forehead. He'd totally forgotten about the game—the game he was supposed to play center striker, the game that was going to start in half an hour! He wolfed down his cereal and toast, gulped a big glass of orange juice, and dashed upstairs to get into his uniform.

His mother drove him to the field. On the way, she gave him a piece of advice.

"Try to put the missing key out of your mind," she said. "Sometimes answers come more easily when you stop thinking about the problem."

"I'll try," Jerry said dismally.

The rest of the Soccer 'Cats were finishing their warm-ups when Jerry slid out of the car.

"Jerry, glad you could make it," Coach Bradley drawled. "Ready to play some ball?"

Jerry nodded weakly. Truth was, he'd never felt *less* ready.

"Great," the coach said. "We're counting on you to fill Stookie's shoes today!"

Hoo boy, Jerry thought. He ran out onto the field.

The 'Cats were playing against the Torpedoes, a tough team to beat. The 'Cats had won the coin toss and had the ball first.

The referee blew the whistle, signaling the start of the game. Jerry took a deep breath, then gave the ball a soft kick. Lou Barnes, the 'Cats' right striker, caught the pass and started downfield.

Jerry jogged along parallel to him. He tried to follow his mother's advice, but he just couldn't get his mind off the missing key.

Where could it be? he asked himself over and

over. Just then, he saw something gleaming in the grass in the field. Hopeful, he steered toward it—

—and missed the return pass from Lou! The ball bounced a few feet away from Jerry, right onto the waiting sneaker of a Torpedo halfback.

"Thanks a lot, pal!" the Torpedo said with a grin. Then she shot the ball skyward. It landed deep in 'Cat territory. The Torpedoes front line swarmed it, as did the 'Cats' four fullbacks. For a moment, no one could see who had possession.

Then it became all too clear. Goalie Bucky Pinter made a dive to the left, but he was too late. The Torpedoes had made the first goal.

As the teams lined up again, Jerry wanted to kick himself. The first play of the game, and he'd botched it! And all for nothing, too. The gleaming thing was just a pop-top from a soda can. He could just imagine what Stookie would have said if he'd been there to see it.

Chapter 9

The rest of the first half was a disaster for the 'Cats. Jerry couldn't seem to get his head into the game. Time after time, he flubbed a pass, had the ball stolen, or missed a chance to score. By the time the ref blew the whistle, the score was Torpedoes 3, 'Cats 0.

Coach Bradley tried to cheer up the 'Cats.

"Okay," he said, "so we've missed a few shots we shouldn't have and let a few go by we should have stopped." He spread his hands wide. "No big deal! Just keep trying your hardest out there. Plug up the holes on

defense and find the holes on offense. These guys aren't so tough." He jerked a thumb toward the water cooler. "Now get something to drink and get ready to blast those Torpedoes out of the water!"

The team gave a shout and headed for the water.

"Jerry, wait a sec," Coach Bradley said.

Jerry hung his head but didn't say anything.

"You know, everyone has off days," Coach Bradley said kindly. "But it seems to me there's something bothering you. You're dragging around out there like a puppet without any strings."

"I'm sorry, Coach," Jerry whispered. He hesitated a moment, then started to explain about the missing key. "Stookie's going to hate me!" he finished with a wail.

"Well, I doubt that," the coach said. "I'm not saying he won't be upset. But it seems you've done all you could to find the key.

You've also done your best to keep an eye on his house and his gerbils. You can't do any more than your best, right?"

"I guess so," Jerry said, suddenly feeling a little better.

"Well, I know so," the coach said. A whistle blasted, signaling the game was about to start again. "And your best is all I'm going to ask you to do. No more puppet, okay?"

"Okay!" Jerry gave the coach a grin.

"All right! Then let's go! Go 'Cats!"

Jerry ran onto the field with his teammates. He was determined not to let the coach down.

"No more puppet," he murmured to himself as he waited for the ref to place the ball in front of him. "No more puppet."

The ref blew the whistle. Jerry toed the ball to Roy Boswick, the left striker. Roy tried to dribble downfield, but he got into trouble right away. Two Torpedo halfbacks double-teamed him.

Jerry was ready. He swooped in, calling for

a pass. Roy shot him a grateful look and booted the ball in his direction.

Jerry caught it cleanly on his instep. The Torpedo halfbacks moved in. Jerry looked up to see if Lou was in the clear. He was. Jerry fired the ball to him.

Lou took off like a rocket. Jerry charged down the field alongside him. One Torpedo halfback covered Lou, the other stayed with Jerry.

Jerry tried to outrun his opponent. But the halfback was quick and stuck to him. Meanwhile, Lou was starting to have trouble.

What would Stookie do now? Jerry wondered. He thought back to the last game. He remembered how Stookie had fooled the defense when he'd stopped dead. Would that work now, too? It was worth a try.

Jerry slammed on the brakes. The Torpedo halfback kept going. Suddenly, Jerry was wide open!

"Here! Send it here, Lou!" he shouted.

Chapter 10

Lou didn't hesitate. His defender was ahead of him, trying to stay between Lou and the goal. He wasn't expecting Lou to pass *backward*. But that's just what Lou did.

Jerry trapped the ball neatly. Then he waited. Sure enough, the Torpedo halfback charged him. With a quick move, Jerry dodged her. He dribbled madly for the goal. The fullbacks tripped all over themselves to get to him. But Jerry remained calm. Out of the corner of his eye, he saw Roy streaking up the sideline.

Jerry waited a beat, then sent the ball rocketing to Roy. Roy stopped it ten feet in front of the goal. He seemed surprised to have the ball, but only paused for a second. With a swift kick, he sent the ball flying into the net for the 'Cats' first goal!

"Wow! Great pass, Jerry!" Roy cried happily. Jerry grinned.

But that was the only goal the 'Cats made. When the game ended, the final score was Torpedoes 3, 'Cats 1.

Jerry was disappointed they hadn't won. But he knew he'd done his best, at least in the second half. The coach thought so, too.

"Glad to see you got rid of the puppet," Coach Bradley said.

"Yup, that puppet is . . ." Jerry's voice trailed off. His jaw dropped and he clapped a hand to his forehead. "That's it!"

Without another word, he grabbed his sweatshirt and ran off the field. He didn't stop running until he reached home—and then it was only to open the door. He pounded up the stairs and into his bedroom.

"Good gracious, where's the fire?" his mother hollered. But Jerry didn't answer. He had crossed the room to his bed, where Otter was sitting.

Breathing hard, Jerry picked Otter up and turned him over. He stuck his hand inside the hole in Otter's back and wiggled his fingers into Otter's arms.

He gave a whoop that brought his mother running. Slowly, he pulled his hand out. In his fingers he held the missing key!

"It must have slipped inside Otter when I put it into the knapsack at Stookie's house!" Jerry cried.

His mother hugged him. "What made you think to look there?" she asked.

Jerry dangled the key from his finger. "It was something the coach said about puppets," he answered. "And in a way, you helped, too."

His mother raised an eyebrow.

Jerry explained. "The one time I wasn't thinking about the key was when I figured out where it might be. Just like you said: Sometimes the answers come to you when you stop thinking about the problem."

Mrs. Dinh ruffled his hair. "Glad to have helped. Now what do you say we go check on those gerbils?"

"You bet!"

SOCCER 'CATS

IS 61 LIBRARY

IS 61 LIBRARY

IS 61 LIBRARY

IS 61 LIBRARY